Picking Berries

Picking Berries

Sealaska Heritage Institute
105 S. Seward St. Suite 201
Juneau, Alaska 99801
907.463.4844
www.sealaskaheritage.org

Design by Nobu Koch.

ISBN: 978-1-946019-10-3

10 9 8 7 6 5 4 3 2

This book was made possible through funds from the US Department
of Education Alaska Native Education Program Grant PR# S356A140060
Raven Reading: A Culturally Responsive Kindergarten Readiness Program. The
contents of this book do not necessarily represent the policy of the DOE,
and you should not assume endorsement by the Federal Government.
Baby Raven Reads is an award-winning Sealaska Heritage education
program promoting a love of learning through culture and community.

Picking Berries

By Hannah Lindoff
with Marigold Lindoff

Illustrated by David Lang

Ah hoo ha hoo berry,
ah hoo ha sing.
Let's pick berries,
the first berries of the spring!

Pink flowers on green leaves,
first brought the bumble bees.

Now the cheerful birds are flitting,
getting berries while we're picking!

So many colors,
yellow, orange, red.
If you like yellow,
I'll eat orange instead.

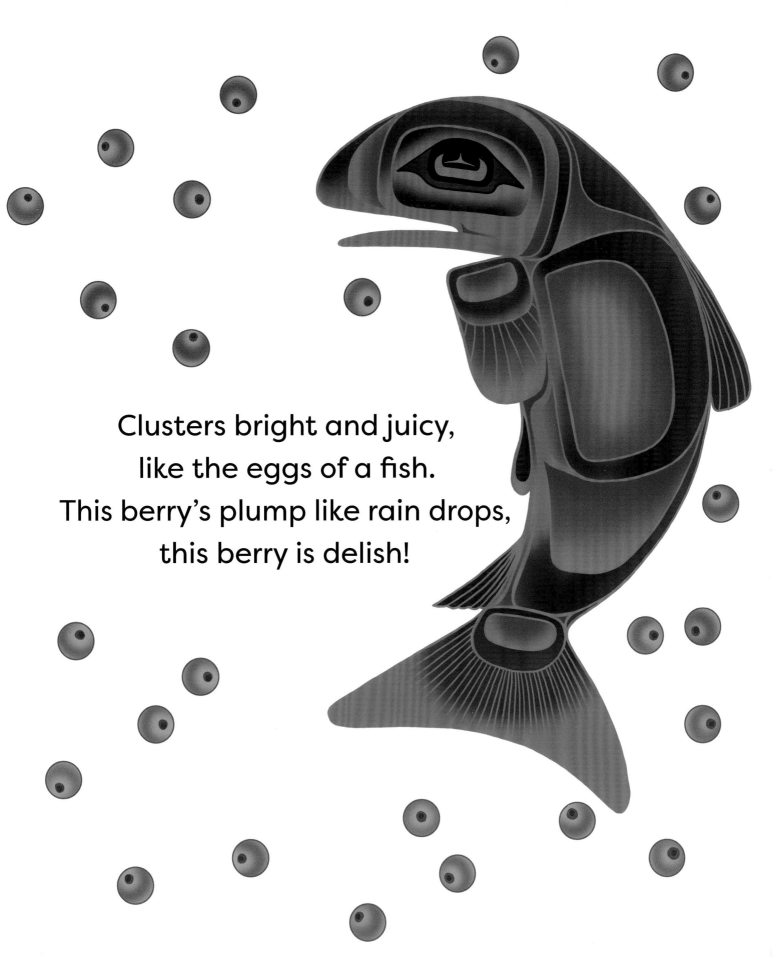

Clusters bright and juicy,
like the eggs of a fish.
This berry's plump like rain drops,
this berry is delish!

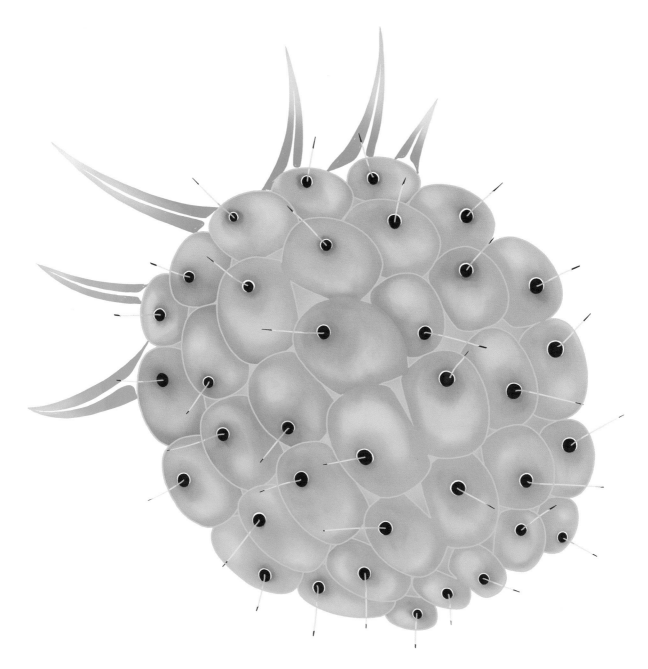

Ah hoo ha hoo berry,
a hoo ha áwaan.
You can call them salmonberry,
me, I say *sḵ'áwaan.**

Ah hoo ha hoo berry,
ah hoo ha hoo.
Going berry picking,
let's get berries me and you!

Find these sweet red berries
down by the beach.
Growing low to the ground,
they're an easy reach.

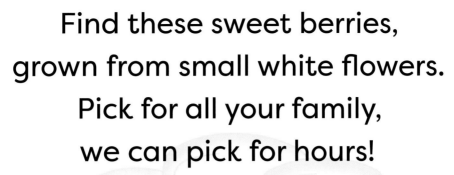

Find these sweet berries,
grown from small white flowers.
Pick for all your family,
we can pick for hours!

The ocean breeze will not slow us,
summer brings so much to show us!

This berry's sweet like sunshine,
this berry's moist like dew,
this berry is my favorite,
berry, berry, I love you!

Ah hoo ha hoo berry,
ah hoo ha hoo ákw.
You can call them strawberry,
me, I call them *shákw!**

Ah hoo ha hoo berry,
ah hoo ha hun.
Ah hoo hoo hoo berry,
picking berries is so fun!

Like a hat on your thumb,
eat these berries one by one!

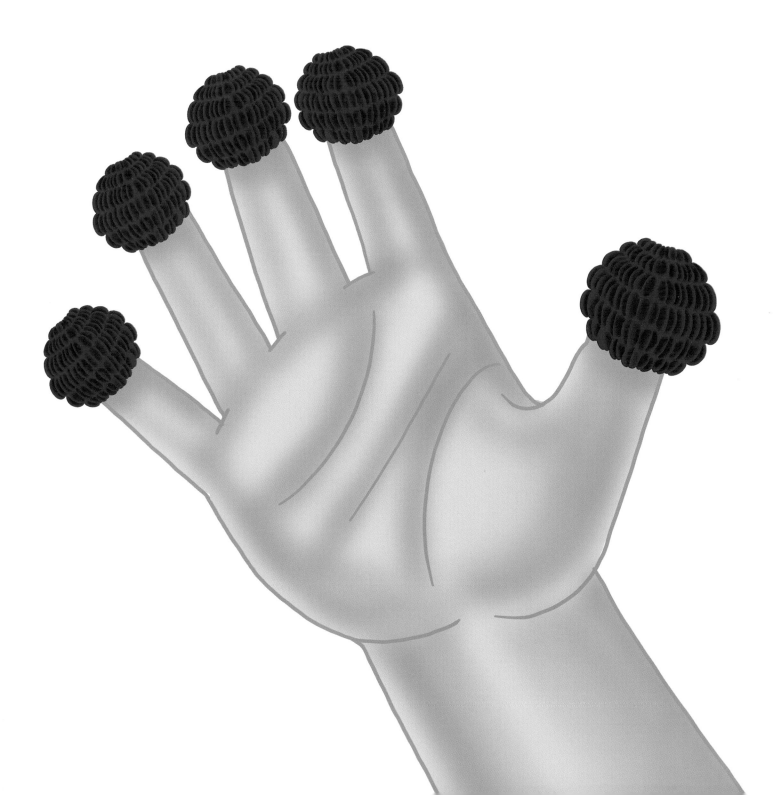

They grow along the forest trails,
here we come with our pails!

A delicate taste, not too sweet,
pick pick, pick, eat, eat, eat!

Berry you're my favorite,
berry ripen, berry grow,
'cause we're coming for you, berry,
berries high and berries low!

Ah hoo ha hoo berry,
ah hoo ha ee̲x'.
You can call them thimbleberry,
me, I call them *ch'ee̲x'.**

Ah hoo ha hoo berry,
ah hoo ha hoo.
Going berry picking,
let's find something blue.

Hanging thick on the branch,
a waving breeze makes them dance.

Or is it a raven, coming through,
picking berries with me and you?!

Purple lips, happy smiles,
berry fields stretch for miles.

Get enough to last through the days,
when night is long and snowflakes play.

Berry, berry, blue and tart,
favorite berry in my heart.

Ah hoo ha hoo berry,
a way hey ha dlá!
You can call them blueberry,
me, I call them *kanat'á.*[*]

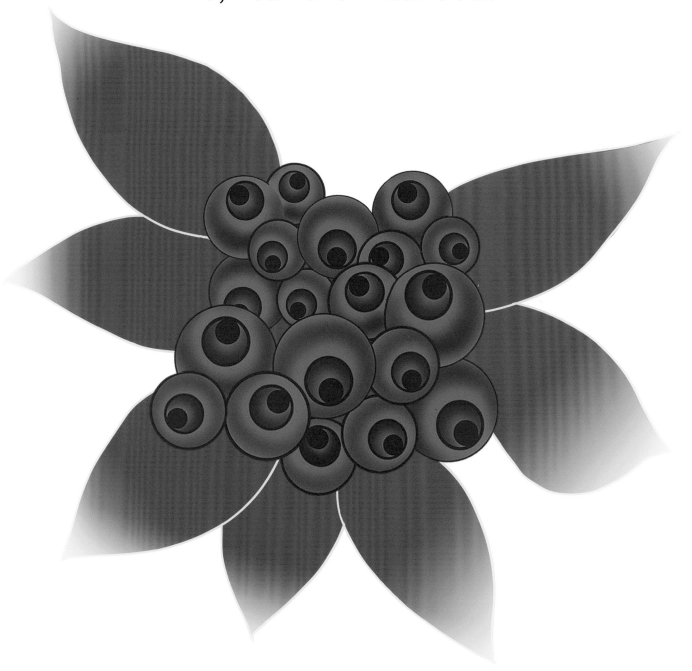

Ah hoo ha hoo berry,
ah hoo ha hoo hey.
Going berry picking,
we'll fill our mouths today!

Beside the road this berry grows
or Grandma's yard in neat rows.

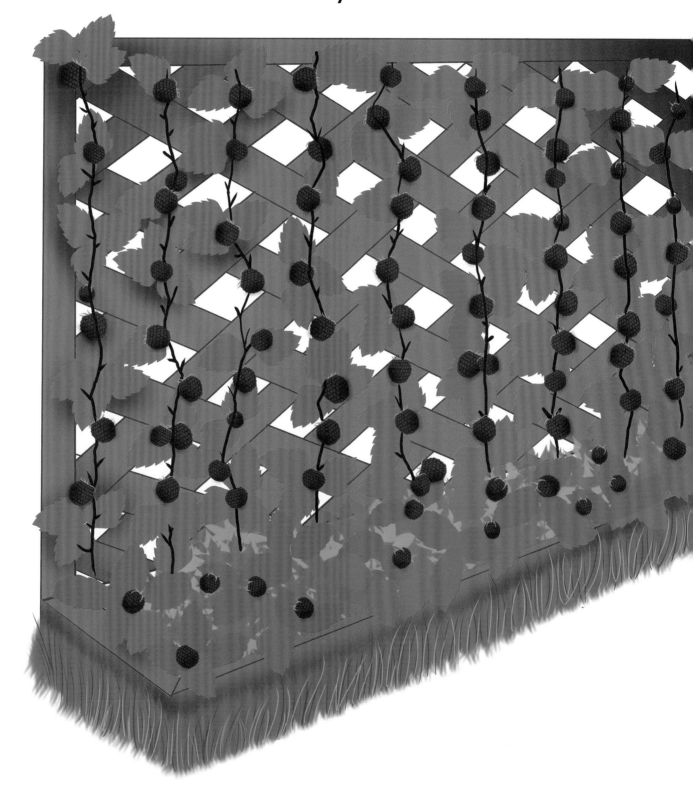

Or hiding spots, secret still,
we'll find these berries, I know we will.

Thorny stems cannot stop me,
little streams are made for hopping!

Berry, berry, soft red berry,
a little fuzzy on my tongue.

The summer's goodness in your seeds,
berry, you're my favorite one!

A hoo ha hoo berry,
a hoo ha ha hoo,
You can call them raspberry,
me, I say *naasu*!*

A hoo ha hoo berry,
a hoo ha hoo!
I love berry picking,
just like I love you!

Berries

in the Tlingit, Haida, and Tsimshian languages

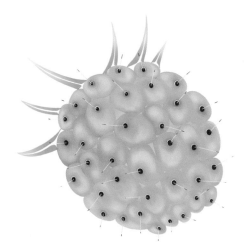

*skʼáwaan is salmonberry
in the Haida language X̱aad Kíl

Lingít: wasʼxʼaan tléigu

X̱aad Kíl: skʼáwaan

Smʼalgya̱x: ma̱gooxs

*shákw is strawberry
in the Tlingit language Lingít

Lingít: shákw

X̱aad Kíl: hildag̱áang

Smʼalgya̱x: ma̱guul

*ch'eex̱' is thimbleberry
in the Tlingit language Lingít

Lingít: ch'eex̱'

X̱aad Kíl: stl'a gudíis

Sm'algya̱x: k̲'oo

*kanat'á is blueberry
in the Tlingit language Lingít

Lingít: kanat'á

X̱aad Kíl: hldáan

Sm'algya̱x: smmaay

*naasu is raspberry
in the Tsimshian language Sm'algya̱x

Lingít: tlék̲w yádi

X̱aad Kíl: sk̲'áwaan gíit'ii (domestic)
              tl'ánts'uud g̲áanaa (wild)

Sm'algya̱x: naasik, naasu

about Sealaska Heritage Institute

Sealaska Heritage Institute is a regional Native nonprofit 501(c)(3) corporation. Our mission is to perpetuate and enhance Tlingit, Haida, and Tsimshian cultures. Our goal is to promote cultural diversity and cross-cultural understanding.

Sealaska Heritage was founded in 1980 by Sealaska after being conceived by clan leaders, traditional scholars, and Elders at the first Sealaska Elders Conference. During that meeting, the Elders likened Native culture to a blanket. They told the new leaders that their hands were growing weary of holding onto the metaphorical blanket, this "container of wisdom." They said they were transferring this responsibility to Sealaska, the regional Native corporation serving Southeast Alaska. In response, Sealaska founded Sealaska Heritage to operate cultural and educational programs.

about Baby Raven Reads

Sealaska Heritage sponsors **Baby Raven Reads**, a program that promotes a love of learning through culture and community. The program is for families with Alaska Native children up to age 5. Among other things, events include family nights at the Walter Soboleff Building clan house, Shuká Hít, where families are invited to join us for storytelling, songs, and other cultural activities. Participants also receive free books through the program.

Baby Raven Reads was made possible through funds from the US Department of Education Alaska Native Education Program Grant PR# S356A140060 *Raven Reading: A Culturally Responsive Kindergarten Readiness Program* running from 2015-2017.

Hannah Lindoff is a life-long Alaskan and adopted member of the T'akdeintaan Clan, from the Whale House in Hoonah. In 2017 Hannah will receive her Master of Fine Arts in creative writing from the University of Alaska, Anchorage. She holds a Bachelor of Arts in English from Mary Washington College and is the author of the children's book *Mary's Wild Winter Feast*. She serves on the Juneau Public Library's Publisher Preview Committee for children's literature and is inspired by her family: her husband Anthony and their two children, Marigold and Otto.

David Lang was born in Juneau and raised in Southeast Alaska until moving to Washington State in his early teens. A commercial artist since 2001, Lang moved back to Juneau in 2009 to open High Tide Tattoo and seized the opportunity to reconnect with his Tsimshian heritage. Since then he has shifted his focus and studies to the Indigenous art of the Northwest Coast, with an emphasis on Tsimshian language and culture.